STARGAZERS to Spaceships

Dear Reader

Thousands of years ago, people looked up at the sky and wondered what might be up there. Imagine what they would have thought if they knew people would one day go into space to see for themselves!

> "FOR THOUSANDS OF YEARS, PEOPLE HAVE LOOKED UP AT THE SKY ..."

It has been over 40 years since people first went to the Moon. It's amazing that astronauts have travelled into space and set foot on Earth's nearest neighbour. It's still amazing to look up at the night sky and wonder about space.

I hope you enjoy your own glimpse of space in this book!

John Parsons

NELSON
CENGAGE Learning™
For learning solutions, visit cengage.com.au

Contents

STARGAZERS to Spaceships

Why do seasons occur?

Early stargazers watched the skies.

humans reach the Moon

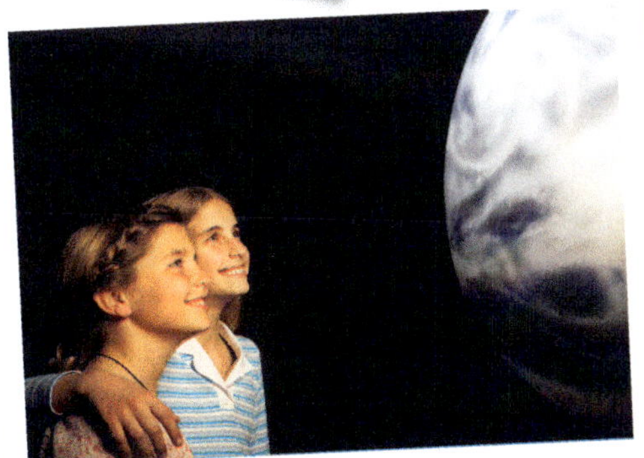

The sky is the limit!

1 Stargazers and Seasons

Early Humans Observed

When the first recognisable humans were on Earth between a few million and 200 000 years ago, their lives would have been ruled by the seasons, as were the lives of their ancestors. It made sense to know as much as possible about the animals and plants throughout the year. Early humans also watched the movements of the Sun, Moon and stars. They would have linked their observations to finding ways to survive.

Early humans evolved from creatures like Australopithecus *(above)*.

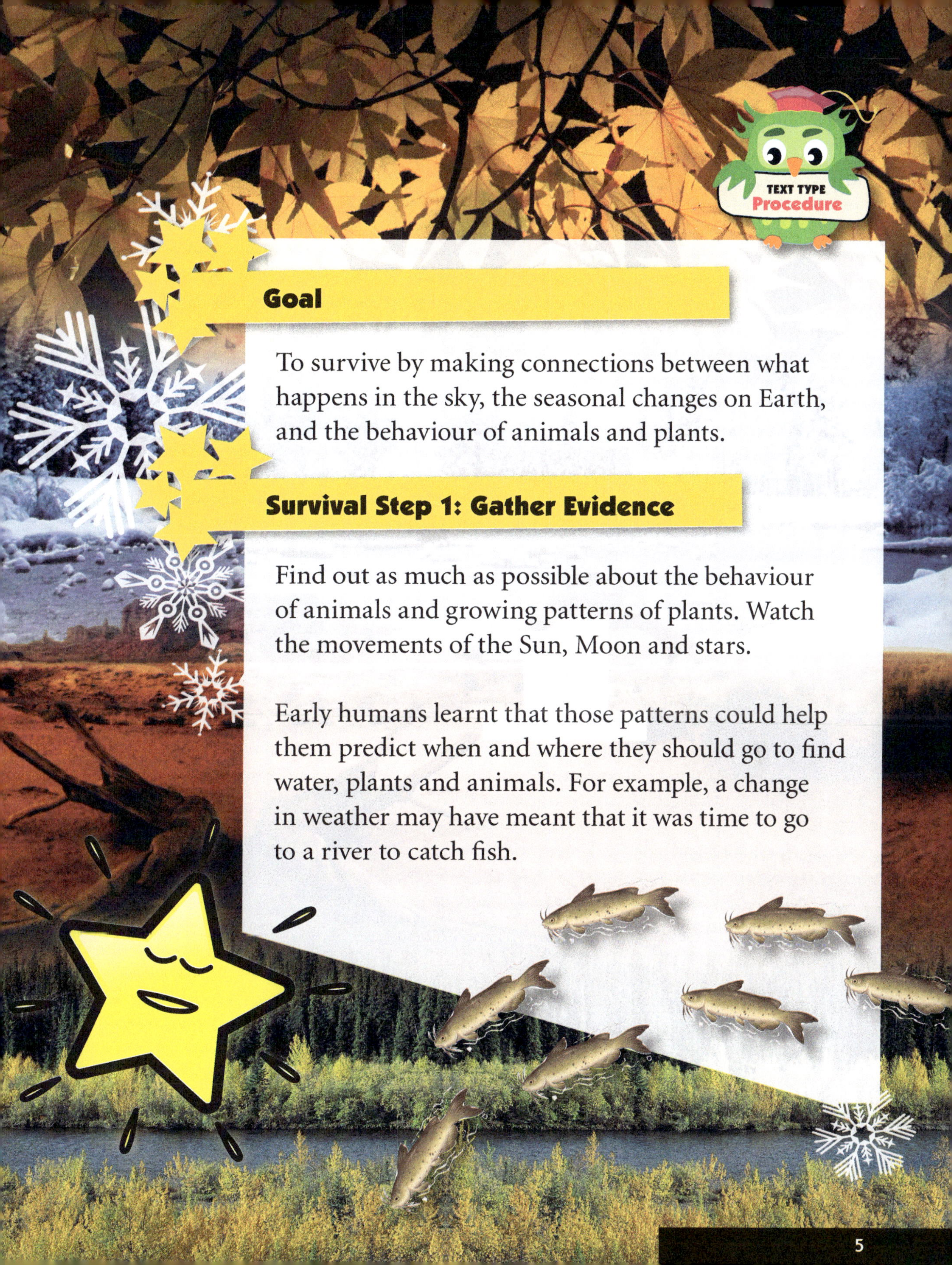

Goal

To survive by making connections between what happens in the sky, the seasonal changes on Earth, and the behaviour of animals and plants.

Survival Step 1: Gather Evidence

Find out as much as possible about the behaviour of animals and growing patterns of plants. Watch the movements of the Sun, Moon and stars.

Early humans learnt that those patterns could help them predict when and where they should go to find water, plants and animals. For example, a change in weather may have meant that it was time to go to a river to catch fish.

Survival Step 2: Make Observations

Look for any patterns between plants, animals, seasonal changes and what happens in the sky. Observe when certain groups of stars or constellations appear. Notice the regular changes the Moon goes through.

Early humans would have observed the way the Sun, planets and stars changed throughout the year. They would have noticed the way the Moon changed each month or so. Then they would have seen how the world around them changed at the same time. Plants grew, flowered, produced seeds and died. Animals had babies, and moved about in search of food and water.

Every year, people observed that plants would flower, fruit and grow seeds at the same times.

Survival Step 3: Test Your Theories

Make theories about why these things happen. Use this information to predict what may happen in the future.

Early humans could have tested their theories by predicting what happened when the Sun, stars or planets were in a certain place in the sky. If early humans were able to find enough food and water, they would have concluded that their theories were correct.

Why Are There Different Seasons?

Earth moves in an ellipse.

We now know that Earth is tilted and travels around the sun in an ellipse (or flattened circle). For part of the year, when some parts of Earth are closer to sun, they are warmer. When others are further away, they are colder. This changing distance from the sun causes the seasons.

Survival Step 4: Remember Your Results

Pass your knowledge on to others so that they can benefit, too.

Early humans would have passed on their knowledge to their children through stories, art, dance and song. They would have remembered the way the world changed with the seasons. They would have used their knowledge to stay safe from dangerous weather, starvation and thirst. From this knowledge, farmers would have known when to plant or harvest their crops; herders would have known when their animals would give birth and make milk; and everyone would have known when to store food to survive.

Observing a Better Time

By about 10 000 years ago, humans had spread across the world. Instead of hunting and gathering food, they began to tame animals. They moved them from one place to another to find fresh pastures. Other humans settled in one place to grow their food.

Although early farmers understood why the seasons changed, they wanted to learn more about time.

An early human settlement was discovered in Skara Brae, in the Orkney Isles, North Scotland.

Problem: What's the Time?

People wanted to know what time it was each day. They wanted to measure each season and divide the year up into months.

If people could find a way to measure time, they could tell exactly how many hours were left before dark. They would also know how many days or months there were until the next season.

Step 1: Observe the Sun

Early humans observed that the Sun cast a long shadow at dawn and dusk. It cast a short shadow at noon. Early "clocks" used shadows to tell the time.

The Sun rises and sets at different places in each season. People would have noticed where on the horizon the Sun rose and set on summer's longest day. They did the same on winter's shortest day.

What could be made to show where the Sun was in the sky and tell the time?

Step 2: Build Time-Keeping Solutions

All around the world, people started to build stone or wooden structures to work as sun clocks. Many people think that Stonehenge, near Salisbury in England, was built to track the movement of the Sun.

Most scientists think that people began building Stonehenge around 10 000 years ago. It is thought that the original builders may have used wooden posts to mark where the Sun rose and set at certain times during the year.

Whatever its purpose, it seems clear that the ancient builders were interested in the movement of the Sun and the Moon.

Shadows cast by the Sun at places like Stonehenge might have been used to mark time and seasons.

Step 3: Make Conclusions About Time

Many people believe there would have been special celebrations to mark the shortest day of the year at places like Stonehenge. This would have been a good time to celebrate as it meant that summer was on its way. The days would gradually grow warmer and longer. This change from a dark, freezing winter to a warm spring and summer was great news!

Social Studies and History

The Mystery of Stonehenge

Stonehenge

Today, many tourists visit Stonehenge and marvel at its size and significance. They try and work out how people could have moved such heavy stones into the area. Many people have theories about why, how and when it was built. Although we know a lot about Stonehenge, there are still many mysteries.

3 Stargazers See Circles

Navigating from Place to Place

As civilisations grew, people found more and more reasons to keep track of how the Sun, Moon and stars moved in the sky.

People started to travel and trade with each other. They realised that they could use the position of the stars to help them find their way. Back then, 12 000 years ago, the star we call Vega always seemed to point north.

In the Southern Hemisphere, the stars of the Southern Cross always helped to show where the South Pole was.

A Sky Map at Sea

Observing the stars was very helpful, especially at sea. Long journeys with no other landmarks would have been dangerous. In Europe and Africa, people traded across the Mediterranean Sea. They used the stars to help them navigate.

In the Pacific and in South America, people travelled huge distances across the Pacific Ocean. They used their knowledge of the stars to find their way from one island to another.

Sailors on early boats, like this Egyptian one, navigated between Africa and Europe by observing the stars.

The North Star Changes Name

The Earth and the stars are always moving, so the star that marks the direction north changes over time, too. The changes happen over a cycle of 26 000 years.

The north star was a star called Vega 12 000 years ago. About 5000 years ago, the north star was Thuban.

Now, Polaris is the star that marks north. In about 5500 years from now, it will be Alpha Cephei.

Polaris

Problem: What's Moving in Space?

People wanted to know more about the movement of the stars, the Moon and the Sun. But being so far away made it very hard to find out more. At that time, no one knew that Earth was moving, too!

The stars of the Southern Cross feature on the Australian (top) and New Zealand (bottom) flags.

Ancient astronomers measured the changing positions of the Moon and stars.

Step 1: Find a Theory

To work out a theory that made sense, people:

- made careful observations of the sky
- drew maps of the stars and planets
- noted the movement of the Sun.

Step 2: Observe the Theory

People could see that the Sun, stars and planets were moving in great circles. Earth seemed to stand still. People came up with a theory that Earth was the centre of the universe, and that everything moved around it.

At the time, this seemed like the best theory. It explained the things people could observe, even if, as scientists worked out later, it wasn't quite right.

Step 3: Theory Tested Later

In 1543, Nicolaus Copernicus, an astronomer, came up with another theory. No one took much notice of his theory until a famous scientist called Galileo agreed with it in about 1614. Galileo got into a lot of trouble because many people disagreed with him. They preferred the previous theory that Earth was the centre of the universe.

Nicolaus Copernicus (1473–1543)

Social Studies

Copernicus

Copernicus was Polish, but he wrote his books in Latin. He was a doctor and a diplomat, and he studied astronomy in his spare time. Copernicus died in the same year that his theory was published. It was said that he woke from a coma, was given his new book to hold, then died peacefully.

pages from Copernicus's book, published in 1543

Does the **Earth or the Sun Move** – or Both?

One of the theories still to be tested was whether Earth moved around the Sun, not the other way round. Was it possible that Earth might not be at the centre of the universe?

Copernicus, and later Galileo, were able to prove that their theory was right.

Galileo (above) also invented the telescope, and showed people how it could be used (left).

Problem: What's Moving Around?

People who watched the movements of the Sun, stars and planets thought they moved around Earth.

Step 1: Make Observations

Copernicus thought of a theory. Later, Galileo agreed with him. They observed the sky very carefully. They drew diagrams and made notes about what they observed through telescopes to try and explain what might be happening. Perhaps Earth could be moving around the Sun?

Step 2: Test Observations

The diagrams, models, maps and charts helped Copernicus and Galileo explain the theory that the Sun is the centre of the solar system.

People could see that this theory was a better explanation. It was Earth and the other planets that moved around the Sun. That movement could explain why the night sky changed.

Step 3: Stargazers Conclude

We now know that everything in the universe is moving, including the Sun and the stars. We also know that Earth is tilted on its axis. This tilting of Earth explains the seasons.

Copernicus's theory and Galileo's research were among the most important steps forward since we started stargazing.

5 Stargazers Imagine Space

Is **Space** Travel **Possible?**

For hundreds of years, people studied the Sun, Moon and the stars more and more closely. Famous scientists discovered many amazing things about our planet, our solar system and our universe.

A Great Novel

Then, in 1865, a French writer called Jules Verne wrote a novel called *From the Earth to the Moon*. He imagined what it might be like for a group of people to travel to the Moon.

People enjoyed reading his book. They also started to think about what would be needed if people wanted to travel to the Moon.

Jules Verne (1828–1905)

Problem: Safe Space Travel
People wanted to travel to and from the Moon safely.

Step 1: Research Space

Scientists needed to study space and the Moon carefully. They knew that the Moon was:

- far away (over 380 000 kilometres)
- without any air to breathe
- without water or food
- constantly moving, just like Earth
- out of reach of almost all forms of communication.

Step 2: Think of Solutions

This meant that space travellers needed:

- a vehicle that could travel huge distances quickly
- accurate navigation
- water, food and air for the journey
- powerful new ways to communicate.

Step 3: Make a Conclusion

In 1865, when people started thinking about space travel, it was impossible. The technology did not exist at that time. However, even if a problem seems huge, if we use our creative and technical skills, we can usually find a solution.

6 Stargazers Travel in Space

Stargazers Solve **Problems**

People have made a lot of progress solving space travel problems from 1865 to today. Scientists, engineers and governments realised that people might be able to travel into space.

By the 1950s, we had developed rockets that could travel huge distances. By the 1960s, it was safer for astronauts to travel in space because:

- Food and water could be preserved safely.
- It was possible to create an artificial environment, with air and heat.
- There were excellent electronic navigation systems available.
- We had early computers.
- We had radio communication.

USA and Russia Lead the Way

But there were still huge problems to overcome. So the United States of America (USA) and the Union of Soviet Socialist Republics (USSR) decided they would be pioneers in space travel.

Over several years, both countries solved space travel problems – many of which are in the chart opposite.

YURI GAGARIN

In 1961 a Russian, Yuri Gagarin, was the first human to travel in space. He was a pilot in the USSR air force. Although he survived the first space voyage, he was killed in an aircraft crash in 1968.

A Russian coin celebrates Gagarin's achievement.

SPACE TRAVEL

PROBLEMS

1
Build a rocket that could fly high enough to go into space and orbit Earth.

2
Launch the rocket successfully.

3
Build a spacecraft that could take a living creature into space.

4
Build a spacecraft that could travel around, or orbit, Earth.

5
Build a spacecraft that could take human beings into space and bring them back.

6
Build a spacecraft that could land human beings on the Moon and bring them back.

SOLUTIONS

1950s
By the early 1950s, the USSR and the USA had huge rockets that could travel into space.

1957
By 1957, the USSR had launched a satellite called Sputnik into space.

1957
In 1957, the USSR sent a dog called Laika into space.

1959
In 1959, a small USSR spacecraft was sent to the Moon.

1961
In 1961 the USSR sent Yuri Gagarin into space and brought him home safely. He was the first human space traveller.

1969
In 1969, the USA landed humans on the Moon. After 200 000 years of stargazing, human beings finally travelled to another world – the Moon.

7 Stargazers Keep Watching!

Eyes on the Sky

Our curiosity about the stars and the universe didn't stop when we landed on the Moon. Radio telescopes, like the one at the Parkes Observatory in New South Wales, Australia, search the night skies for signs of new stars and galaxies. Below is a timeline of space travel developments since the 1970s to today.

Since 1971

Crews have been doing experiments in space stations.

Skylab was an American space station. When it crashed in Western Australia in 1979, the local council fined NASA $400 for littering!

Since 1977

Since its launch in 1977, the Voyager 1 spacecraft has travelled over 16 billion kilometres from the Sun. It is now the most distant human-made object from Earth. Voyager's radio signals take 14 hours to reach Earth.

Since 1990

Since its launch in 1990, the Hubble Space Telescope has sent us amazing images of the universe. It can see far beyond anything that a telescope on Earth can see.

the Hubble space telescope

Since 2000

Since 2000, the International Space Station has had a full-time crew as it orbits Earth. People in space programs are planning to send humans to other planets, such as Mars. They are searching for life on other planets.

Thanks, Stargazers!

Now that we are more technologically advanced, so much more is possible in space. But we still owe an enormous amount to those first stargazers.

They taught us that it is important to understand our environment. And they taught us that observation is the first step towards solving problems.

Thanks to their imagination, we are no longer stargazers, but space travellers!

Index

Glossary

astronomers	Scientists that study space and the objects in it (such as planets, stars and galaxies)
astronomy	The science and knowledge of space and the objects in it
axis	The central point around which something turns (like an axle)
diplomat	A person who represents their country or government in a foreign land
engineers	People who work with machines and technology to create solutions to problems or needs
landmarks	Places or features in a landscape that can be easily recognised by people in that area
observatory	A place where space is studied, or observed, usually through telescopes
theories	Ideas of how things work that attempt to explain natural events or phenomena